Make Way
for
DYAMONDE
DANIEL

Make Way for DYAMONDE DANIEL

Nikki Grimes

illustrated by

R. Gregory Christie

SCHOLASTIC INC.
New York Toronto London Auckland
Sydney Mexico City New Delhi Hong Kong

ISBN: 978-0-545-22241-9

Text copyright © 2009 by Nikki Grimes.
Illustrations copyright © 2009 by R. Gregory Christie.
Published by Scholastic Inc., 557 Broadway, New York, NY 10012,
by arrangement with G. P. Putnam's Sons, a division of Penguin
Young Readers Group, a member of Penguin Group (USA) Inc.
SCHOLASTIC and associated logos are trademarks
and/or registered trademarks of Scholastic Inc.

12 11 10 9 8 7 6 5 4 3 2 1   9 10 11 12 13 14/0

Printed in the U.S.A.   40

First Scholastic printing, October 2009

Design by Katrina Damkoehler
Text set in Bembo Semibold

For Maleah—N.G.

For Sandra Green—R.G.C.

Contents

Dyamonde Daniel
was a gem waiting to be
discovered . . .

The World of
Dyamonde Daniel

Dyamonde Daniel

Meet Dyamonde, a
third-grader with wild-crazy
hair and a zippy attitude.
She's super smart and has
met just about everyone in
her new neighborhood. The
only thing she's missing is
a best friend.

Free

The new boy! He's super
tall and growls at everyone.
Is he as rude as he seems, or
is there more to him than that?
Dyamonde is determined to
figure him out.

The Three T's

Tanya, Tylisha and Tameeka—known as the Three T's—are nice enough to Dyamonde at school, but she's not really part of their group.

Dyamonde's mom

Dyamonde's parents are divorced, so it's just Dyamonde and her mom these days. Her mom is proud of her daughter's awesome brainpower, but she isn't about to let Dyamonde get away with anything!

New Kid

Dyamonde Daniel was a gem waiting to be discovered. Just ask her.

So what if she had wild-crazy hair and was skinnier than half a toothpick? On the inside, she was extraordinary. Plus super smart. As a matter of fact, she had more brains in her tiny little pinky than most kids had in their whole entire bodies.

When Dyamonde was a little kid, she had to keep that to herself. Why? 'Cause her mom said her being super smart was a family secret. "So you can't tell anyone," said her mom.

Puleeze! thought Dyamonde. *Give me a break!*

Back then, she believed her mom, though. What do you want? She was just a kid.

Then one night Dyamonde heard her mom talking on the

telephone, telling someone how smart her daughter was. That was the end of *that* secret! Now everybody knows how smart she is. Dyamonde still doesn't always go around saying how smart she is, though. It's not nice to brag.

One morning, in her third-grade homeroom, Dyamonde was feeling down.

If I'm so smart, thought Dyamonde, *how come I've been in this new school three whole weeks and I still don't have a new best friend?*

Dyamonde didn't have time to

figure it out because her teacher, Mrs. Cordell, clapped to get everybody's attention.

"Class," said Mrs. Cordell, "we have a new student joining us today. Please say hello to Free."

"Hello, Free," everyone said, like robots.

And what did that boy do? He grunted!

Puleeze! thought Dyamonde. *How rude!*

"Free just moved here from Detroit—it is Detroit, right?" asked Mrs. Cordell.

Free grunted again. Mrs. Cordell, who Dyamonde decided was being *way* too nice, pretended not to notice.

"I hope you will all make Free feel welcome."

Dyamonde shook her head. She already knew she didn't want to have anything to do with that boy. So, of course, he took the seat right in front of her.

Oh, brother, thought Dyamonde. *Now I have to stare at his fat head every day.*

Well, his head wasn't fat, really. It was a nice head, covered with tight brown braids. His head was hard to see over, though, because he was so tall.

When the lunch bell rang, even though he didn't deserve it, Dyamonde invited Free to sit with her. She knew how lonely it felt to be the new kid in school. But instead of being grateful, he mumbled, "Leave me alone."

Dyamonde sucked her teeth. *Too rude!* thought Dyamonde. Aloud, she said, "Suit yourself," and went on to the lunchroom without him.

The seats in the lunchroom filled up fast. Not that it mattered to Dyamonde. She already knew where she was going to sit.

Dyamonde got in line and bought a milk to go with the peanut butter and jelly sandwich she'd brought from home, then took a seat with Tanya, Tylisha and Tameeka—the three T's. They weren't about to let Dyamonde into their little group, but they were nice enough to her at school. Sitting at their table during lunch made her feel a little less alone.

One plus three equals four, thought Dyamonde. *Four's a nice, sturdy number, like a table with four*

legs, or a square, all cozy and zipped up on all four sides.

Dyamonde liked even numbers. In fact, Dyamonde liked numbers, period. Math made sense to her. Numbers were neat, and easy, and solid. Not like English, which was full of rules that changed all the time. Yes, math was best. Math was something you could always count on. Well, mostly.

For a long time after her mom and dad got divorced, Dyamonde hated math because all she could see was subtraction. Mom's voice minus Dad's. Two for breakfast instead of three. Monday night TV minus the football. It just didn't feel right, at first. But things were a little better now. Dyamonde plus her mom equaled two, and two was a nice even number, and even numbers rule. So, while the three T's were not her real friends, sitting with them at lunchtime gave Dyamonde a break from feeling like the odd number she was at school the rest of the day. After all, who wants to feel odd?

Dyamonde couldn't help but

notice that Free sat at a table in the back, all by himself. *Talk about odd,* thought Dyamonde.

She just shook her head.

Boys.

Lonely Girl

Dyamonde was happy to go home that afternoon. The next day was Saturday, which meant no Rude Boy and no feeling lonely in the school yard. Plus, on Saturdays she could sleep as late as she wanted. And she might as well. She didn't have anything else to do these days. Well, she had homework, but that didn't count. She always had homework.

Dyamonde turned the key in the front door of her apartment building. She was supposed to go straight to her neighbor's on the second floor and wait there till her mom came home from work. Instead, she slipped into the tiny apartment she shared with her mom, dropped her books on the couch and grabbed her favorite photo album from the bookshelf.

Where is it? thought Dyamonde, flipping the pages.

There!

She turned to a page of pictures of herself with her best friend, Alisha. Her old best friend. The one Dyamonde had to leave behind in Brooklyn when her parents got divorced and her mom moved them to this new place in Washington Heights.

Dyamonde sighed. More subtraction. Her least favorite kind of math.

In the old days, Alisha had been part of Dyamonde's cozy foursome: herself, her mom, her dad, plus Alisha made four.

"I miss you," Dyamonde said to

the girl in the photo. She missed her dad too. And their old apartment where she had her own room. Here, she had to sleep on a pullout sofa. It wasn't half bad, though. It was plenty roomy enough for her to stretch out on, even sideways. Plus, her mom had offered her the bedroom, but Dyamonde had said no. She figured moms should have their own bedrooms. Even so, it was nice having a bedroom with your own desk and stuff. Dyamonde sighed a second time. Truth is, she missed all kinds of things.

Not that her new neighborhood was boring or anything. 147th Street and Amsterdam Avenue was pretty much bursting with life. There was the House of Beauty, where ladies got their hair curled and colored. There was Hal's Hair Shack, where men went for haircuts. There was a Laundromat for folks who didn't have washing machines in their basements, and a bunch of different restaurants. Some sold Chinese takeout, some sold fried chicken, and some sold nothing but barbecue. There was a great candy store, a newspaper stand and a flower stand. As far as

Dyamonde could see, the neighborhood had just about everything you could ever want.

Sure is nothing like the quiet old neighborhood we used to live in, thought Dyamonde. The Brooklyn brownstones had been nice enough, but they were mostly filled with old people on Dyamonde's block.

This new neighborhood was alive, like Dyamonde. The avenue was always busy with all kinds of people coming and going. Dyamonde figured if she sat perfectly still on her stoop, or stared out her window long enough, the whole world would pass by. Ladies in crisp nurse's uniforms catching the uptown bus to Columbia Presbyterian Hospital. Men and ladies in suit jackets catching the bus to fancy offices downtown. There were kids like Dyamonde playing stickball or handball against a building, or walking to school like Dyamonde did every day.

The avenue suited Dyamonde just fine. Still, that didn't keep her from missing the friends she left behind in Brooklyn.

What she did *not* miss were the loud fights her mom and dad had been having the last few years. Them not living together was definitely better.

Dyamonde ran her finger over Alisha's photo, then closed the album and put it back on the shelf.

Suddenly, Dyamonde's shoulders sagged.

Saturdays are a waste, thought Dyamonde. *No more treasure hunts with Alisha. No more sleepovers. No more pictures together.*

Dyamonde grabbed her books and dragged herself downstairs to her neighbor's apartment to wait for her mom. "What's the matter?" asked her neighbor, Mrs. King.

"Nothing," Dyamonde said with a sigh. Mrs. King patted her on the head like a puppy, the way she always did. For once, Dyamonde didn't mind.

By the next morning, Dyamonde felt better, especially when she woke up to a familiar smell.

"Dyamonde!" called her mom. "Your pancakes are getting cold."

Dyamonde smiled. She liked having her mom all to herself on

Saturdays. Plus there was one more good thing about Saturdays.

Pancakes!

"Coming, Mom!"

Here Comes Rude Boy

On Monday, Dyamonde tried to slip out of the house without a jacket. It was the end of September and still warmish. She had on her red T-shirt, jeans and a blue vest with rows of red, white and blue buttons sewn on the pockets. She called it her Independence vest, and she didn't want to cover it up with a silly jacket. She'd sewn those buttons on with her own hands, and she wanted everybody to see them.

"Bye, Mom," said Dyamonde, almost out the door.

"Jacket," said Mrs. Daniel. Dyamonde rolled her eyes but went back to her closet.

Mothers, thought Dyamonde.

There was no point in complaining. It's not like she was going to be late for school. Since school started, she'd been leaving early each morning. She didn't have any special friend to walk to school with, and she didn't want to be reminded by seeing groups of other kids walking together. She felt left out enough as it was.

Once she got to her home-room, Dyamonde read over her homework while she waited for class to start. She looked up when the bell rang, just in time to see Free stomp into the room.

Oh, brother, thought Dyamonde. *Here comes Rude Boy.*

She decided to ignore him, which was easy enough to do in class because he was quiet as a mouse. He never raised his hand.

He never asked any questions. And when the teacher called on him to read, he slouched in his seat and made up some excuse not to.

Dyamonde shook her head. *I know that boy can read,* thought Dyamonde. *Just last week, I caught him reading a book in the school yard after lunch.* Nobody *reads in the school yard unless they just plain* like *to read. So why is he making out like he doesn't?* Dyamonde shook her head again. *And why do I even care? Forget him.*

Dyamonde turned her attention back to Mrs. Cordell.

28

Outside of homeroom, Free was harder to ignore. He stomped everywhere, growled at anyone who spoke to him, and kept bumping into kids because he didn't look where he was going.

Two days in school, and he had almost everybody scared of him already. And he didn't even have to try hard. He was the tallest kid in the third grade, almost as tall as a sixth-grader. When you're that big, all you have to do to scare somebody is show up and say boo!

Free never said boo, but he

looked mad all the time, and that was enough to scare most of the kids. Dyamonde wouldn't have cared except Free was being mean to kids who were too little to speak up for themselves.

Dyamonde wanted to do something about it, but she didn't know what.

Maybe Mrs. Cordell can help, thought Dyamonde.

One afternoon, she hung around after the last bell so she could talk to her teacher in private.

"Mrs. Cordell," said Dyamonde.

"Yes, dear?"

"What's the matter with the new boy? With Free?"

"What do you mean, sweetie?" Mrs. Cordell called everybody "sweetie."

"How come he's mad all the time?"

"I don't know, Dyamonde. Why don't you ask him?"

Dyamonde practically choked at the very thought.

"Never mind," muttered Dyamonde.

I like Mrs. Cordell and all, thought

Dyamonde, *but that's crazy. No way am I asking Rude Boy anything.*

Dyamonde knew there was something wrong with him, though, and she figured one of these days she'd find out what.

That day came sooner than she expected.

Chicken Nugget Tuesday

One Tuesday—it was chicken nugget day, to be exact—Dyamonde was sitting with the three T's when Free stomped into the lunchroom, fists clenched, not looking where he was going—again. He bumped into Jordan, this tiny third-grader, and mumbled, "Out of my way, squirt." Poor Jordan shook so hard, he dropped his tray. Free just kept going, got his own lunch and slammed the tray down on a nearby table.

That's it, thought Dyamonde. *I'm tired of seeing that boy scare the living daylights out of everybody in sight. Time somebody stood up to him.*

Dyamonde walked straight up to Free and said, "What is your problem?"

Free looked up from his plate, startled.

"Who says I got a problem?"

"You have *got* to be kidding!" said Dyamonde, with one hand on her hip. "See that little kid over there?" With her chin she pointed to Jordan, who was still on his hands and knees, chasing his spilled chicken nuggets after dropping his tray.

"*You* did that!" said Dyamonde.

Free, suddenly looking sheepish, mumbled, "Sorry."

"Humph!" said Dyamonde. "You should be. Now, tell *him*."

Free thought she was kidding, but Dyamonde glared at him, hand still on her hip. He could tell she wasn't going to go away anytime soon.

"Sorry, kid," Free yelled, loud enough for Jordan to hear. Only then did Dyamonde return to her own table.

Dyamonde kept her eye on Free after that. Whenever she caught him growling at someone, she'd scowl at him. If she heard him yell at little kids, she'd step in front of them, cross her bony arms and stare Free down until he said he was sorry. After a few days of this, Free did his best to stay out of everybody's way, especially Dyamonde's. For some reason he couldn't quite figure out, he didn't want her mad at him.

Later that week, Dyamonde's mother sent her across the avenue for some Chinese takeout. On the way back, Dyamonde found Free sitting alone on the stoop of the building on her corner. She had heard he lived nearby, but this was the first time she'd seen him.

"Hey," she said as she passed.

As always, Free just grunted.

Dyamonde shook her head. "Now, if you were smart," said Dyamonde, "you could have said,

'Hay is for horses.' If you were *smart*."

"What's so smart about that?" he shot back.

Dyamonde turned around and walked back to his stoop. There was something bugging this kid, and Dyamonde was going to find out what. Nobody could be that mean, all the time, for no reason, could he?

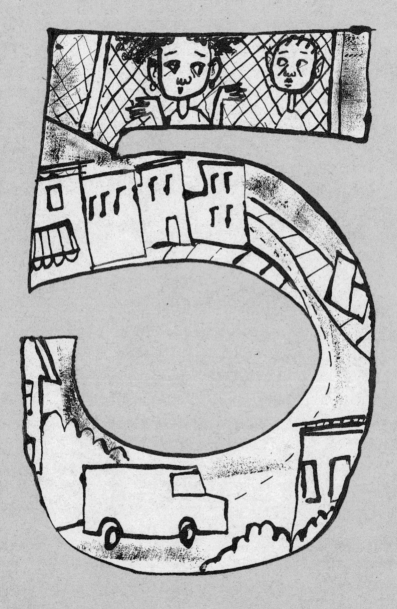

Dyamonde Digs for Answers

"Who are you so mad at?" asked Dyamonde.

The question caught Free off guard.

"What?"

"Who are you so mad at?"

"Who said I was mad?"

"Oh, puleeze! All you do is stomp around and glare at people, even teachers, and I have not seen one person do anything bad to you since you got here. Not *one*. So who are you mad at?"

Dyamonde's words were sharp as needles, and Free felt like a balloon that she had just poked a hole in. All the air came whooshing out, and instead of looking angry, Free just sort of sagged.

"I don't know," said Free, in a tired voice. "I'm mad at my folks. At my dad, mostly. He lost his job and made us move here, and I had to leave all my friends behind."

Dyamonde thought about her

old neighborhood, and her old friends. The face of Alisha came swimming up before her eyes, and Dyamonde had to swallow hard. She wasn't mad at Mom for making them move, but she understood how Free could be mad at his dad.

"Okay," said Dyamonde. "You've got a right to be mad—but not at people you don't even know."

Free sighed. "I guess you're right."

"Of course I'm right. I'm *always* right," said Dyamonde. The way she said it made Free smile.

"What's your name again?" he asked.

"Dyamonde, with a *y* instead of an *i* plus an *e* at the end. And yes, I know. I must be a diamond in the rough, 'cause I'm plain as coal, blah, blah, blah. I've heard it all," said Dyamonde, rolling her eyes to the sky.

"Kids tease you about your name all the time?"

"Yeah."

"How do you stand it? I hate it when kids tease me about mine."

Dyamonde shrugged. "It used to bug me when I was little. I

even changed my name to Diana for a week. But Dyamonde sounds so much more beautiful, and I figured anybody who made fun of it was just plain silly. Besides, there are way worse things in life than being teased about your name. Anyway, who would tease you about Free?"

"Nobody. But my last name is Freeman. And my first name is Reed."

"What's wrong with that?"

"When's the last time you met some kid named Reed, especially a black kid? People always say to me,

'Hey Reed, what are you reading?' Or 'There goes Reed, reading again.'"

"Got it."

"So I just use Free, short for Freeman. Only my family calls me Reed."

"Well, I like it—Reed."

"Don't—"

"Don't worry," said Dyamonde, rising from the stoop. "I won't call you that when other people are around. Well, gotta get this food home before it gets cold. See ya."

"See ya," said Free.

Dyamonde took a few steps,

then turned back. "One more thing. Quit being so touchy about your name," said Dyamonde. "Believe me, I've heard way worse!"

With that, Dyamonde ran to her building and disappeared through the door before Free could speak. She liked getting in the last word. And why shouldn't she? Isn't that what all smart people do?

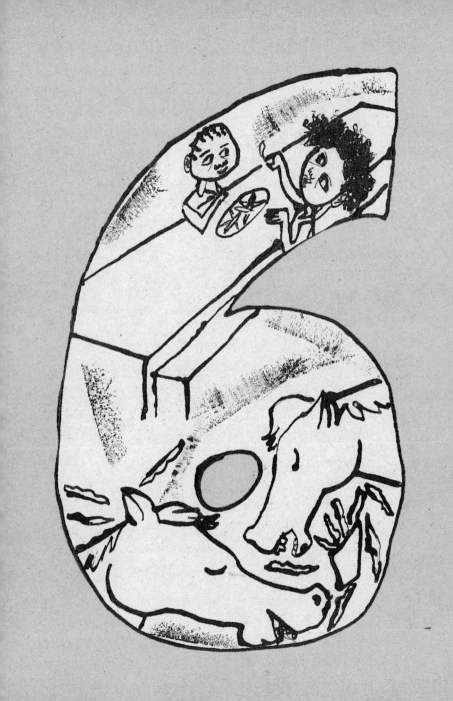

Hay's for Horses

The next day at lunch, Free did his usual thing. He carried his tray to the empty table farthest from the entrance and sat alone. He wasn't alone for long, though.

"Hey," said Dyamonde, sliding in across from him.

"Hay is for horses," said Free.

Dyamonde smiled.

"You sure you want to sit here? You see how everybody's looking at you like you're crazy."

Immediately, Dyamonde stood up and faced everyone who was staring in her direction.

"What?" she asked. "Cat got your tongue?" Each person seemed to be waiting for somebody else to speak. When no one did, they all turned away and went back to eating their lunch.

Dyamonde sat back down.

"Can I have some of your fries?" asked Dyamonde.

"Wow," said Free. "You're amazing."

"What?"

"You really don't care what people think."

"About what?"

"About sitting with me. About anything."

"Why should I?" asked Dyamonde. "I know what I think, and that's enough."

Free just shook his head.

"You can't do things or not do things just 'cause somebody else thinks you should. I mean, what if they're dumb as a rock and you're paying attention to them? That's silly. Anyways, can I get a couple of fries or not?"

Free pushed the plate of fries toward Dyamonde and was quiet for a long while. She sure gave him a lot to think about.

Side
by
Side

The next morning, when Dyamonde came downstairs, she found Free on her stoop, waiting for her. He didn't growl at her the way he did before, but he was still sour looking.

"How come you're always so grouchy in the morning?" asked Dyamonde.

"You would be too if you had to share a bunk bed with your baby brother and he was yappin' all the time. I need earplugs just to get some sleep."

"Don't you get used to it?"

"I haven't so far. Back in Detroit, I had my own room."

"Still. You got a bedroom. That's something."

Free shrugged. "I guess." He was going to complain some more about how crowded it was in his grandma's tiny apartment, but something told him not to.

When school let out that day,

Dyamonde found Free hanging around the entrance. She headed home and he fell in step with her.

"So you know I like to read," said Free.

"Me too," said Dyamonde. "And I like basketball."

"So do I. And baseball."

"And handball."

"Handball?"

"I'll teach you," said Dyamonde. "What's your favorite color?"

"Blue. Yours?"

"Red. Best color in the universe."

"I collect marbles."

"Rocks."

"You got a home computer?"

"No," said Dyamonde.

"Me neither."

"We moved here this summer. You?"

"One month ago."

"I live with my mom. She and my dad got divorced."

"I live with my mom, dad, brother and grandmother. We moved here when my dad lost his—oh, that's right. You already know that."

Dyamonde smiled. "You're so lucky," she said.

"Huh?"

"You have a brother *and* a grandmother. My grandparents are all dead."

"Yeah?"

"Yeah. My mom says I'm as stubborn as my grandmother, and just as mouthy. I wish I'd gotten to know her for myself, see if Mom was right. Having grandparents would have been cool."

"Well," said Free, "you can share mine. And you can have my brother, Booker. What a pain!"

"That's what everybody says about their brothers and sisters.

But sometimes, I wish I had one to talk to."

Free didn't know what to say to that.

Dyamonde looked up just as they were passing House of Beauty. An old lady sitting under the hair dryer stared at her through the window. Dyamonde waved.

"That's Ms. Gracie Lee, nosiest person on the block. If you do something and you don't want your mom to know about it, don't do it in front of Ms. Gracie. By the time I get home, Mom'll know I've been walking with 'that Freeman boy.'"

"But how does she know—"

"She knows ev-er-ry-thing," said Dyamonde.

Next, she waved to a young mother pushing a baby in a carriage, with two more little ones trailing behind. The lady at the flower stand smiled at her, and she nodded at the man at the newsstand who called to her, "Hey there, Dyamonde."

"You know all these people," said Free. It wasn't a question, but his voice was full of wonder.

"Sure. You will too, after a while."

"I don't know," said Free. "We may not be here that long. Depends on my dad. You know. If he finds a job. I mean, *when* he finds a job."

Dyamonde touched Free's arm. "He will find a job, Free. I'm sure of it. But my mom says even when he does—"

"She knows about me and my dad? You talk about us?"

"Well, yeah. You're my friend. Why wouldn't I?"

Free relaxed, let the word *friend* wash over him.

"Right."

"Anyway, even when he gets a

job, it might take a while to save up money to move. Plus, maybe he'll just move you guys to an apartment close by. That way, you can stay in the same school, see? So why not get to know everybody in the neighborhood. You might be here for a long time."

At least I hope so, thought Dyamonde. But she kept that thought to herself.

Before she knew it, they had reached her building. She waved good-bye to Free and ran inside.

Good-bye, Alisha

Every day after becoming friends with Free, Dyamonde left for school at the same time as everyone else, walking side by side with Free. They ate lunch together, played together in the school yard and even passed funny notes to each other in class.

The last days of September

turned quick as the pages in a good book. October blew in cool, but with her new best friend, Dyamonde hardly felt it.

Dyamonde still missed Alisha, just not all the time anymore. And Free was much less grouchy than he used to be. He stopped growling at everybody and even surprised the teacher one day—in a good way.

It was reading time, and Aaron, the boy in front of Free, had finished reading his paragraph. Mrs. Cordell skipped over Free because he never wanted to read out loud.

"Dyamonde," she said. "Could you pick up the next—"

Free raised his hand.

"Yes, Free?" asked Mrs. Cordell. "What is it?"

"Can I read next?"

Kids were poking each other and laughing. Even Mrs. Cordell looked shocked, but she nodded yes.

Turns out, Free could read better than almost anyone! Everybody was surprised. Except for Dyamonde, that is.

"Show-off," Dyamonde whispered when Free was done. She was smiling when she said it.

That evening, Dyamonde took out her photo album and turned to her favorite picture of Alisha.

"I still miss you," she said to the picture. "But guess what? I've got a best friend here too. His name is Free."

The next day was Saturday, and Dyamonde knew exactly how she wanted to spend it. She picked up the telephone and dialed Free's number. Mrs. Freeman answered, then handed the phone to Free.

"Hey, it's me," she said when he picked up. "I'm going treasure hunting tomorrow. Want to come?"

"Sure," said Free.

Dyamonde smiled, happy to have a new adventure to look forward to, and happy to have someone to share it with.

Dyamonde plus Free equals two, thought Dyamonde.

Even numbers rule!

Born and raised in New York City, **Nikki Grimes** began composing verse at the age of six and has been writing ever since. She is the critically acclaimed author of numerous award-winning books for children and young adults, including Coretta Scott King Award winner *Bronx Masquerade*, Coretta Scott King Honor winner *The Road to Paris* and *New York Times* bestseller *Barack Obama: Son of Promise, Child of Hope* (illustrated by Bryan Collier). In addition to a Coretta Scott King Award and four Coretta Scott King Honors, her work has received accolades such as the NCTE Award for Excellence in Poetry for Children, *Booklist* Editors' Choice, ALA Notable, Bank Street College Book of the Year, *Horn Book* Fanfare, American Bookseller Pick of the List, Notable Social Studies Trade Book, NAACP Image Award Finalist, and the Golden Dolphin Award, an award given by the Southern California Children's Booksellers Association in recognition of an author's body of work. She lives in Corona, California.

Visit her at www.nikkigrimes.com.